Mayhem and Midnight Tea

A Bel Harbor Cozy Mystery

Emma Lenn, Author

My clean and wholesome
Cozy Mystery books
are family friendly.
12-year-olds, seniors,
and any age in between.

INTRODUCTION

Thank you for reading my introductory novella:'

"Mayhem Murder and Midnight Tea,"

A Bel Harbor Cozy Mystery

Follow this fantastic trio:

Amateur Sleuth Rachel Karr,

Detective Luke Farley, and

Teen Maddie Farley

as they come alive and

sleuth their way through my books.

See you in the next book

"Books, Burglars, and a Body"

Emma Lenn, Author

Mayhem Murder and Midnight Tea, A Bel Harbor Cozy Mystery

All of my books are strictly works of fiction.

They are not meant to represent

any real person, place, or thing.

My characters and stories

are brought to life

solely through your imagination.

TABLE OF CONTENTS

CHAPTER ONE

With an insatiable curiosity, Rachel Karr, a woman of exuberance and lightheartedness, had earned a reputation as the village sleuth. Armed with keen observation skills and an uncanny ability to connect seemingly unrelated dots, Rachel had solved her fair share of perplexing mysteries, all while maintaining an air of cozy charm.

After completing her education at a nearby college, Rachel began her career as a social worker. However, the demands of the job, with its extensive travel requirements, gradually wore her down. Eventually, she relinquished the position to return to her beloved hometown, spending the last five years caring for the elite residents of Bel Harbor.

Nestled among the trees and along the seaside, Bel Harbor exudes an air of affluence and community. Its cobblestone streets harkened back to a bygone era, winding past luminous mansions, quaint cottages, a park, canopied stores, and aromatic bakeries. The villagers moved through their usual routines with practiced ease.

But on this particular day, a different kind of mystery brewed in the tranquil heart of Bel Harbor.

Rachel despised her current role as caretaker. The five months she had spent tending to Mrs. Kincaid had left her questioning her affinity for caregiving. Living with Mrs. Kincaid Monday through Friday night and most of Saturday, Rachel relished her weekends at home with her mother, Claire. Their cottage, near the edge of Bel Harbor, exuded a charm that mirrored Rachel's childhood memories, lovingly decorated by her mother.

Aware of the uncertainty that awaited her each day, Rachel kept her morning routine brief. Her shower, dressing, and light breakfast were swiftly completed, with the most time dedicated to taming her long, curly locks. After a cursory glance in the mirror to approve her appearance, Rachel intentionally sauntered to her car.

Clutching the steering wheel, Rachel released a brief scream before exhaling deeply and starting the engine. The drive to the Kincaid mansion was short, Bel Harbor being a small village. Yet with each passing moment, Rachel's heart grew heavier.

Mrs. Kincaid proved to be the most infuriating and cantankerous person Rachel had ever encountered. Proud, irritable, and downright rude to anyone who crossed her path, Mrs. Kincaid showed no gratitude toward Rachel, despite her devoted attention to her every whim throughout the day. Yet, for all her unpleasantness, Mrs. Kincaid ensured Rachel was handsomely compensated for her services.

Parked in front of the Kincaid house, Rachel stared at the imposing front door through the passenger window, entertaining thoughts of fleeing and never looking back. However, having lived in Bel Harbor most of her life, she couldn't fathom existence elsewhere.

Summoning her courage, Rachel retrieved her bag and stepped out of the car. As she approached the front door, she fumbled through her purse for the house keys. Yet, to her surprise, the door stood unlocked, slightly ajar. Rachel hesitated before slowly pushing it open and entering, a pang of unease prickling her skin.

"Mrs. Kincaid?" Her voice echoed in the stillness as she closed the door behind her. Ordinarily, Mrs. Kincaid would respond with a sharp retort, dismissing her presence. But today, an eerie silence hung heavy in the air, sending a shiver down Rachel's spine. With each step toward the staircase, she felt the weight of foreboding settle upon her, though she failed to grasp its significance until later.

An old painting, a cherished possession of Mrs. Kincaid, hung askew on the wall beside the stairway—a subtle clue Rachel overlooked in her haste. Given Mrs. Kincaid's physical limitations, she couldn't have pushed it aside herself. Oblivious, Rachel ascended the stairs, calling out once more into the silence.

"Mrs. Kincaid?" Her voice trembled slightly, met only by the echo of her own footsteps. A sense of dread gnawed at her insides as she approached Mrs. Kincaid's room.

Rachel opened Mrs. Kincaid's door. A muffled gasp escaped Rachel's lips as she saw the chilling scene before her. Mrs. Kincaid lay motionless on the cold tile floor, her eyes and mouth frozen open in a grotesque parody of life. Beside her sat the empty wheelchair, a stark reminder of her condition.

With trembling hands, Rachel reached out to touch the cold skin, seeking any sign of life, but found none. Panic gripped her chest, threatening to suffocate her.

Nausea churned in Rachel's stomach, threatening to overwhelm her. She stumbled backward, her mind grappling with the surreal horror unfolding before her. With trembling hands, she turned and fled down the stairs, desperate to escape the suffocating grip of fear. She needed to fight back the nausea long enough to make the 911 call.

Outside, she leaned against her car, her breaths coming in ragged gasps as she dialed 911. Each moment felt like an eternity as she waited for someone to answer, her voice shaking as she relayed the grim discovery.

A woman picked up immediately, and Rachel heard, "911, what's your emergency?"

"This is Rachel Karr. She's d-dead, Mrs. Kincaid, I went into the house just now, and she's dead." Rachel was shaking.

"Mrs. Kincaid?" It was a tight-knit village where everyone knew everybody. "Stay put, Rachel. The police are on their way."

Rachel dropped the phone, her body trembling with shock and disbelief. The reality of the situation began to sink in, each passing second dragging her deeper into the abyss of despair. She kept replaying the scene in her head, and each time, the horror intensified. The last time she saw Mrs. Kincaid was on Saturday night, so it was hard to comprehend the bluish dead body upstairs to be the vibrant woman she was recently with.

Half an hour later, the wail of approaching sirens pierced the stillness of the morning. Rachel looked up to see the Bel Harbor Police van pulling up outside the Kincaid house. As Officers James and Williams emerged, she hurried to meet them, her hands shaking uncontrollably.

"Good morning, Miss Karr," they greeted solemnly.

"Good morning, Officers. I arrived a few minutes ago and couldn't get an answer from Mrs. Kincaid. I went upstairs and saw her in her room. She's... she's dead. I can't believe—" Rachel's voice faltered, choked by emotion. She had never seen a murdered body.

"It's okay, Miss Karr," Officer James interjected, offering a reassuring pat on her shoulder. "An ambulance and the Forensic team are on their way. We'll go look around and wait for them.

They had barely stepped into the house when the team and ambulance arrived, drawing curious gazes from the neighbors who had begun to peek out of their windows.

Knowing that news of Mrs. Kincaid's death would soon spread, Rachel decided to call Anne first. As the medical officials rushed into the house, Rachel went to her car to make the call.

Anne answered after a few rings. She was the niece of Mr. Kincaid, late husband of Mrs. Kincaid, and the only relative Rachel had ever talked with or seen. Her voice, always tinged with a smile, sounded distant yet comforting over the phone.

"Hello, Rachel." Anne's voice floated over as she took the call. Anne always spoke like she was smiling, which was a trait Rachel found endearing.

"Hi, Anne." There was a slight pause.

"Rachel?" Anne's tone held a hint of concern. "Is everything okay? Is Aunt alright?"

For the first time that morning, tears sprang to Rachel's eyes. She had been trying so hard to keep herself together, but she hated the hope in Anne's voice when she asked about her Aunt.

"I'm sorry, Anne, there is no easy way to say this; I found her dead in her room this morning." Tears slipped down Rachel's face. Anne sucked in a breath. "Oh my Gosh." Her voice shook with emotion. "Has she been taken for tests? Have you told Jessica? I have not seen her for quite a while."

"The Police, Forensic team, and ambulance are here. No, I don't have Jessica's contact information, I don't know her." Rachel replied, her voice strained with sorrow. She could not explain or understand these bursts of emotion.

"I'll call her and get back to you." Anne's voice shook severely. Rachel was convinced she would have a good cry after the call.

As they ended the call, Rachel's thoughts turned to Jessica, Mrs. Kincaid's estranged daughter, who had never reached out in the five months Rachel had worked for her. Waiting for the medical officials to carry Mrs. Kincaid's body to the ambulance brought a wave of finality, reminding Rachel of life's unpredictable nature and the fleetingness of human connections.

Soon the medical officials appeared, carrying Mrs. Kincaid's body on a stretcher toward the ambulance. Rachel shut her eyes to block out the scene while biting back tears and nausea.

Mrs. Kincaid was never a great person to her, but there was a finality in the situation that upset Rachel. It further drove home how fickle life was. You could see someone today and never see them again.

A sudden knock against her window jolted Rachel, causing her to startle. Peering out, she saw Officer James standing outside, gesturing for her to roll down the window. "I didn't mean to startle you," he apologized as she complied. "But we need the house keys to secure the premises."

"Of course," Rachel replied, retrieving the keys from her dashboard and handing them over.

"We will also need your statement," Officer James continued, taking the keys. "It shouldn't take too long, just a formality. Are you okay with that?"

"Okay." Rachel nodded, though a wave of dizziness washed over her, making her sway slightly.

"Are you alright?" Officer James asked gently. "Perhaps it's best if you go with the ambulance. They can give you a quick check at the clinic."

"I'm okay. Just a little shaken." Rachel shook her head as they walked to the Police van. "I think I'll be fine," Rachel insisted.

"It's just... I can't shake this feeling of guilt. I'm with Mrs. Kincaid all week, why did something happen when I'm not there?"

"Don't blame yourself," Officer James reassured her, his voice calm and soothing. "It's not your fault."

As they reached the van, another officer awaited them, holding a pad and pen. "It wasn't your fault," he echoed Officer James' sentiment. "Based on our initial assessment and the condition of her body, it seems likely Mrs. Kincaid died from poisoning. The medical examiner will conduct tests, and we should have more definite answers in a few days."

But just as the officers were about to climb into the van, they exchanged knowing glances with Rachel, realizing the nightmare was far from over.

CHAPTER TWO

"I'm sorry for calling you so late, Rachel." Anne's voice sounded nasal and strained, as if she'd been crying. Rachel's heart ached for her. Since discovering Mrs. Kincaid's body yesterday, Rachel had been unable to find any peace or rest; she could only imagine how Anne, as an actual step-relative, was coping.

"I've been trying to reach Jess since you told me the news yesterday, but I only managed to get through to her this morning," Anne continued, her voice catching. "Both she and I are out of the country. I'm terribly sorry, Rachel. It'll take me at least a week to make it back to Bel Harbor. Is that alright with you?"

"Sure." Rachel replied sympathetically. "It will probably take that long for Mrs. Kincaid's body to be released anyway."

"Please keep me updated with everything that's happening. I wish I could be there immediately."

"No problem; when there's news, I'll call you."

"Thank you so much, Rachel. You've been so helpful."

"Anytime."

As the call ended, Rachel tried to refocus her attention on the television, but her mind kept wandering. Anne's call had served as a painful reminder that Mrs. Kincaid was truly gone.

Initially, Rachel had believed her death to be natural, but Officer James' mention of possible poisoning had thrown her into a tailspin of doubt and unease.

Poisoned? The word echoed in Rachel's mind, sending shivers down her spine.

Rachel jumped. Her thoughts were abruptly interrupted by a knock on the door. Startled, Rachel approached cautiously, wondering who it could be. It seemed too early for the neighborhood kids to be selling cookies or lemonade. Peering through the eyehole, she was met with the sight of a handsome man in his late thirties standing outside her door. He was impeccably dressed in all black, exuding an air of confidence and authority.

The man raised his hand to knock again, but Rachel swung the door open with a frown. "Hello." She looked him over. "Can I help you?"

"Good morning, Miss Karr."the man replied, flashing a badge from his wallet. "I'm Luke Farley, a detective with the Bel Harbor Police Department."

Luke looked at this slim woman with great interest. Her dark red hair, hazel eyes, and smooth skin were stunning.

And Rachel, at the same time, was thinking that this man was intriguing. Those dark brown eyes many women dream of having.

Rachel scrutinized the badge before meeting his gaze again. "I have never seen you before."

The detective smiled and rocked back on his feet, a friendly expression on his face. "Do you know everyone in Bel Harbor?"

"After thirty-three years here, I certainly do know almost everyone. It is a small town,"Rachel smiled.

"You're righ,." he nodded. "I moved to the neighborhood about two months ago to fill this position at the Police Department."

"Oh." Rachel stepped aside, gesturing for Luke to come into the house. "Please, come in."

"Thank you," Detective Farley stepped through the doorway and made a beeline for the couch. Rachel waited until he was seated to offer him refreshments. "Will you like tea? Or water?"

"I'm fine, thank you." He took a pad and pen from his pocket, silently communicating his intention to Rachel. She took the sofa opposite him and folded her arms in her lap.

"I'm sure you know why I'm here," Detective Luke said. "I have a few questions concerning the death of Mrs. Kincaid." His fingers were poised over the pad, ready to write.

Rachel nodded, her stomach churning with anxiety. "Have the test results come back?" she asked, recalling Officer James' mention of a couple weeks' wait.

"No, the results are not out. But there's evidence suggesting Mrs. Kincaid ingested poison. We're still investigating the specifics."

"My goodness," Rachel's heart sank at the confirmation.

"Do you stay here at the house, or do you commute?"

"I stay here," she answered. "I have a room upstairs, just down the hall from Mrs. Kincaid's."

"When was the last time you saw her?" Detective Farley continued.

"Saturday evening," Rachel recalled. "I leave on Saturday nights, so I wasn't here yesterday."

Rachel, memories flooding back, thought about when she walked out of the house after leaving Mrs. Kincaid in her room upstairs on

Saturday. Rachel helped her get bathed, dressed in a nightgown, and ready for bed.

Mrs. Kincaid could slide in and out of her wheelchair onto other chairs and bed. She was not completely helpless. With that and help from Mr. Arnold, when he was around, she was capable of being alone on Sunday. She had all the conveniences she would require in her suite.

"Would you mind accompanying me back to the house?" the detective requested. "You might notice something out of the ordinary."

Rachel hesitated, a mix of reluctance and curiosity swirling within her. Her heart pounding, she glanced at Detective Farley, who had already sprung to his feet." Alright," she finally agreed. Her air was thick with tension and uncertainty." Let me grab my coat."

Could there be some mysterious clues in the Kincaid house that she had missed the first time? She was about to find out.

CHAPTER THREE

A few minutes later, Detective Farley and Rachel cruised towards the Kincaid mansion. Rachel, uncomfortable with the silence in the car, broke it. "So, Luke, how are you finding Bel Harbor?"

"I can't complain," Luke replied, steering down the quiet road. "It's a bit quieter than what I'm used to, but I'll adapt."

"I've never been outside Bel Harbor besides a nearby college." Rachel said, shaking her head. "Maybe one day, I'll plan a trip."

"I encourage that," Luke said. "But trust me, you're not missing much except noise and pollution."

Pulling to the curb, they saw a figure huddled over Mrs. Kincaid's door. "Who's that?" Luke asked, turning off the engine.

"That's Mr. Arnold." Rachel exited the car and walked briskly to the front porch where the figure was still standing, a hand on the door. "He's a close friend of Mrs. Kincaid."

As Rachel neared the door, she realized that Mr. Arnold was sobbing. He was an elderly gentleman who lived next door. Rachel was always in awe at the easy friendship between him and Mrs. Kincaid, especially since Mrs. Kincaid never got along with anyone else. Maybe they bonded over their shared trauma of having no family visitors.

Mr. Arnold also lived alone, and he didn't have a caregiver. "Mr. Arnold." Rachel touched his shoulder.

The man turned, his cheeks stained with tears. Rachel's heart broke. "I heard the news this morning," he said in a broken voice. "What happened? I wasn't there for her..." he broke down in tears, and Rachel hugged him. Seeing a seventy-year-old man cry was not on her to-do list this morning. But, being a compassionate woman, she wanted to comfort him.

Rachel thought—Mr. Arnold must go home, and away from this chilling scene.

"I'm so sorry, Mr. Arnold." Rachel patted his back, guiding him towards his cottage. "Let me take you home." His substantial, quaint cottage looked tiny next to Mrs. Kincaid's mansion.

Luke remained in the car while she slowly walked Mr. Arnold back to his house. She returned to the Kincaid home when she was sure he was okay. Luke was already standing at the door.

"So who exactly is this Mr. Arnold?"

"I told you, the closest friend to Mrs. Kincaid. He usually calls or comes over often to visit Mrs. Kincaid. He helps her with things that she could not do or wanted only him to do."

"Something wrong with his back?" Luke asked, noting Mr. Arnold's posture.

"Not sure. A lot of things happen later in life, Detective Farley."

"Please call me Luke," he said, turning to Rachel as he put the key in the lock.

When the door opened, Rachel could smell the familiar scent of lavender, Mrs. Kincaid's favorite.

She stepped through the doorway, immediately noting the brown cup on the coffee table. She walked towards it curiously and peeked inside to see the remains of black coffee at the bottom.

"What is it?" Luke came to stand beside her.

"This cup wasn't here when I left on Saturday," Rachel said, inspecting it closely.

"She could have made coffee," Luke started, but Rachel interrupted him.

"No, she couldn't have," Rachel countered, leading him to the kitchen. "I make her coffee every morning, and she can't reach the island."

Examining the coffee maker, Rachel pointed out, "See? It's plugged in, and Mrs. Kincaid couldn't access it."

"Yes?" Luke nodded slowly, not getting her point.

Rachel explained further, "Mrs. Kincaid is confined to a wheelchair. She cannot reach the island. I make her coffee every morning when I am here. Orange juice is kept in her room when I'm not. There are all the conveniences required to keep her comfortable until Monday morning."

"Could it be leftover from the coffee you made on Saturday?"

"No. That's a unique paper cup, possibly from Mr. Pete's. I've never seen it here."

"Oh." Luke muttered, jotting down notes. "Someone must have been here then."

"Definitely. And this coffee is black." Rachel returned to the living room to peek into the cup. "Mrs. Kincaid drinks her coffee with lots of milk and never drinks leftover coffee, so I'm confident this isn't her drink. I would never give her anything in a paper cup. She had a favorite teacup she insisted on using for her coffee and tea."

"Hmm, puzzling," Luke thought as he wrote down her statements.

Rachel began to grow uneasy. She remembered the day she discovered Mrs. Kincaid hated black coffee. New on the job, she had poured the black coffee straight out of the pot and gave it to her. Mrs. Kincaid took one sip and spat it back out; her expression turned into a big frown. "I never drink black coffee. Another thing, I always want my coffee or tea in my china teacup," she said in her trademark scowl. "That's the first thing you learn if you want to remain here!"

Yes. Rachel was sure Mrs. Kincaid had nothing to do with the cup on the coffee table. The paper coffee cup belonged to someone who visited here over the weekend.

"I'll have to take the coffee cup along with me. See if we can get something out of it. DNA, fingerprints, anything."

"No problem," Rachel said, fetching a fresh plastic bag from the kitchen.

Luke thanked her, but he pulled out an evidence bag and carefully placed the cup inside.

As Luke secured the cup, Rachel shifted her focus to the rest of the living room. She scanned the area, searching for anything amiss. She knew precisely how she had left things on Saturday night. With Mrs. Kincaid's limited mobility, there was only so much she could alter in the room.

"Does anyone know you don't stay with Mrs. Kincaid on Sundays?"

"It's pretty common knowledge. Everyone knows everything about everyone in Bel Harbor," Rachel remarked as she stopped by a massive frame on the wall. It held a picture of Mrs. Kincaid in her younger years, a rare smile adorning her face.

Rachel wondered what had changed for the woman captured in the frame. Rumors circulated in the village about an accident, but Mrs. Kincaid never spoke of it. Rachel knew better than to pry.

"You didn't know I was in town, though. Maybe words don't spread fast enough," Luke returned.

Rachel bounced back to reality. "To be fair, I haven't been paying much attention to anything lately. Mrs. Kincaid became quite demanding; it was hard to focus on anything else. But I'm sure I'll hear all about you soon, in the coffee shop, in the saloon..." she trailed off, her gaze shifting to a painting beside the stairway.

If there was anything in this house that Mrs. Kincaid prized the most, it was this painting.

She would spend hours on the landing, just staring at it. Rachel always wondered what the woman saw. To her, it was just a random abstract artwork. To Mrs. Kincaid, it was something more.

Not only would the woman stare at it, but she would also demand that Rachel spend a lot of time cleaning, dusting, and polishing the vast frame, a chore that she disliked.

Another thing Mrs. Kincaid did was to ensure that after cleaning, Rachel spent more time correctly positioning the painting. Mrs. Kincaid had her measure it. The artwork must always hang 100cm from the left and 100 cm from the right, smack in the middle of the wall. She kept a tape measure nearby.

Today, something caught Rachel's eye.

The painting, usually meticulously aligned, hung askew to the left, as if someone had pushed it. Rachel furrowed her brow. Mrs. Kincaid wouldn't have been able to reach it from her wheelchair, and she never took on such tasks herself. Mr. Arnold usually helped her.

Luke appeared beside her suddenly. "What are you looking at? Did you find something else?

"Detective Farley," Rachel said, her voice taut with urgency. "Someone was definitely in here. We have to find out who." She relayed her thoughts to him.

"Not we, Rachel, me. You are just a witness," he said, but then added more softly "Please stay out of it."

In that moment, Rachel realized she hadn't been searching for clues to a murder that fateful Monday morning. Her mind had been preoccupied with the impending week with Mrs. Kincaid. She had overlooked the open door, the foreign cup of black coffee, the washed and meticulously clean teacup placed on the wrong shelf, and now, the skewed painting. These details, so obvious now, had eluded her in the beginning.

Rachel's thoughts were consumed by the sight of Mrs. Kincaid's lifeless body. As her thoughts lingered on Mrs. Kincaid's motionless form, her mind raced with a whirlwind of questions and fears. Was this a sinister act? Who had silenced Mrs. Kincaid forever?

CHAPTER FOUR

"You are right." Luke nodded, glancing at the wheelchair before returning his gaze to Rachel. "There's no way a woman who relies on this wheelchair could have reached that painting."

"Exactly." Rachel's pulse quickened. She had uncovered two crucial clues, igniting momentum in the investigation. With Luke Farley now convinced that someone had trespassed in the house, Rachel felt a surge of validation.

"Do you know of anyone who might have wished harm upon Mrs. Kincaid?"

The question caught Rachel off guard, her eyes snapping up to meet Luke's. "What?"

"It's a blunt question," Luke clarified, raising his hands in a placating gesture. "But we need every lead we can get. So, do you have any suspicions about who might have wanted her dead?"

Rachel sighed, sinking back into the couch. "It could be anyone, really," she admitted after a moment's contemplation. "Mrs. Kincaid had a falling out with almost everyone in town."

"Really?" Luke was surprised.

"Yes." Rachel nodded. "Even our neighbors. She's had run-ins with them, their kids, and doesn't hesitate to involve the authorities.

Mrs. Kincaid could be abrasive, rude, and downright unpleasant. She always seemed to be annoyed."

"Did any of this happen recently?"

"Oh, not really. People tend to steer clear of her due to her volatile nature. But wait..." Rachel's expression shifted as a recent altercation came to mind. "There was a dispute not long ago, but I can't imagine Sheila or Pete being capable of this. They—"

"Let me be the judge of that, okay?" Luke smiled. "Tell me about this fallout."

"Hmm…" Rachel straightened up. "She had a major falling out with Miss Sheila, a fellow member of her knitting group. There's a friendly knitting competition coming up, and Sheila was chosen to represent Bel Harbor. Mrs. Kincaid wrote a letter to the group, exposing some of Sheila's personal secrets. As a result, Sheila was removed from her position, and Mrs. Kincaid took her place."

"That's quite underhanded," Luke remarked with a furrowed brow.

"She was, indeed, underhanded, without speaking ill of the deceased. She was determined to represent the group at any cost, even if it meant betraying confidences."

"So…Sheila might have had a motive for wanting Mrs. Kincaid out of the picture." Luke made a note of that. "But you don't think she's capable of harming anyone."

"No," Rachel shook her head firmly. "Sheila is a kind-hearted person. She wouldn't harm a soul."

"Who is Pete you mentioned earlier?" Luke inquired.

"You know the Wonder Express in the village? Pete and his wife Berry own it."

""The bakery, right?"

"That's the one. It's a popular spot for snacks and drinks in Bel Harbor. They are open long enough for after work meals."

"I know. I stop by to get snacks from there almost every night." Luke agreed.

"Who doesn't? It is the best bakery in the village. Pete and Berry run it," Rachel continued. "Last week, Mrs. Kincaid demanded doughnuts and chamomile tea, even though Pete's bakery was closed for the night. She wanted him to open up, prepare her tea, and deliver the order to her, nearly at midnight."

"Pete declined politely, suggesting she wait until morning, especially since he was already close to home. Mrs. Kincaid took offense. By the time Pete woke up the next day, she had already contacted the landowner of the bakery site. The price she paid was exorbitant, some say it was ten times its value."

"Sounds like she had quite a fortune," Luke remarked..

"More than enough. But Mrs. Kincaid enjoyed flaunting her wealth and power over others for no good reason."

"So I take it Pete wasn't thrilled about having her as his new landlord?"

"He stormed over to her house to confront her. She assured him she'd have his bakery torn down within a few weeks. And if you knew Mrs. Kincaid, you'd know she never made empty threats."

"Alright," Luke noted down the information. "So Pete also had a motive."

"He's also a genuinely good person," Rachel added.

"I'm sure,"he acknowledged, closing his notebook and rising to his feet. " Would you like a ride home?"

Rachel stood as well, eager to leave the somber atmosphere of the house behind. "No, but if you're headed to town, I'd like to stop by the bakery."

"I assume it's to buy yourself something sweet and not to ask questions."

"Oh, yeah, absolutely. All this talk of doughnuts has me craving Pete's treats."

"Your involvement in this case ends here, Miss Karr." Luke stated firmly, meeting her eyes. "You've helped us tremendously, but anything more would only hinder the investigation."

"Trust me, I have no urge to snoop around. The sooner I forget about this, the better.

Detective Farley dropped Rachel off at the bakery twenty minutes later. Before parting ways, they exchanged phone numbers, with Rachel promising to call if she recalled anything else.

As Rachel entered the bakery, she was greeted by Pete's warm smile behind the counter, which reminded her of her recent conversation with Luke.

"Hey there, Rachel," Pete called out cheerfully. "Glad to see you. Come on over."

Grinning, she walked towards him. "Good to see you too, Pete. What's smelling so delicious today?"

"Oh, you've got to try our strawberry fudge cake. It's divine." Pete slid open the display window and cut a generous slice, placing it on a plate before handing it to her. Rachel couldn't resist inhaling the sweet aroma. "Oh, Pete, this smells amazing."

"I've heard it tastes like heaven, too. Try it."

Pete watched expectantly as Rachel took a forkful and savored the explosion of flavors in her mouth, prompting an involuntary moan of delight. "Wow, this is incredible. I'll take three slices, please."

Chuckling, Pete served her the requested slices. "On the house," he said, his expression sympathetic. "I'm sorry about Mrs. Kincaid."

Luke's earlier analysis of Pete as a suspect lingered in Rachel's mind, making Pete's condolences feel somewhat surreal. "Thank you, Pete. I appreciate it."

"No worries, Rachel."

Carrying the plate, Rachel opted for a seat by the window, seeking solace in the view outside and some distance from the other patrons. She needed space to gather her thoughts.

Across the street, she observed older gentlemen gathering around a newspaper stand, engaging in light-hearted banter. However, her peace was interrupted by a voice beside her.

"Hello."

Rachel turned, frustrated at being disturbed but relaxing a little, when she saw a young girl with long blonde pigtails standing beside her, with a school bag in hand. "Oh, hi."

"May I sit with you?" The girl asked with a nervous smile.

"Sure." Rachel gestured to the seat across from her. She wanted privacy but didn't mind sharing the space with the young girl.

"I'm Maddie." The girl extended her arm across the table, and Rachel shook her hand. "It's nice to meet you, Maddie. I'm Rachel."

"Sorry to disturb you," Maddie said, opening a textbook on the table. "This is my favorite seat."

"You must come here often?" Rachel cut a piece of the cake and ate it.

"Every afternoon, after classes. I come here to do my homework."

"Why not do your homework at home?"

"Because I don't like to be alone while I do it." Maddie shrugged. "I like privacy but don't want to be alone. Does that make sense?"

"Perfectly," Rachel chuckled to herself. "I feel that way sometimes."

Rachel remained quiet while Maddie sat across the table to finish her homework. She turned towards the window again, but her attention was no longer on the older gentlemen across the street but on her previous meeting with Luke Farley.

"Are you alright? You're frowning hard." Rachel felt a light touch on her arm and jumped. Maddie immediately pulled away, hurt.

Rachel reached out to hold her. "I'm so sorry, Maddie. I became lost in my thoughts."

"It's okay," Maddie smiled, patting Rachel's arm. "My Dad does that sometimes. He gets lost in thought, but I understand because he's always solving cases."

"What sort of cases?" Rachel took another bite of her cake.

"He never talks about it." Maddie shrugged. "So I've stopped asking."

Rachel sighed. "I could use your dad's advice right now," she joked. "There's also a case that's troubling me."

"I'm my father's daughter." Maddie wiggled her brows and puffed her chest. "I can advise you. What's this about?"

"Like your dad, I cannot talk about it. Not really."

"Even better." Maddie nodded. "That's my specialization."

Rachel laughed. "Okay. Hit me with it.

"I don't know what case is troubling you," Maddie began. "But I approach problems like puzzles." She reached into her bag and pulled out a torn newspaper page, revealing a crossword puzzle.

"When I'm stuck on a puzzle, it consumes me," Maddie explained. "I can't shake it off, whether I'm at school, the park, or anywhere else. It's always on my mind."

"So, what's your strategy?" Rachel inquired, intrigued.

"Now, I try to start a puzzle when I have enough time to finish it. I don't quit until it's all done, no matter how tough it gets. If I get interrupted, I come back to it as soon as I can."

At first, Maddie's explanation didn't make much sense to Rachel. But as she pondered it further, the concept clicked. She couldn't shake off her concern about Mrs. Kincaid's unresolved death. Despite telling Detective Farley otherwise, she remained deeply invested in the case.

Returning to Mrs. Kincaid's house to search for more clues seemed like the logical step. After all, she had already uncovered the significance of the coffee cup and the askew painting on the wall. There might be more to discover. She turned to Maddie with a broad grin. "Maddie!

Rachel walked around the table and hugged Maddie, who giggled. "You're brilliant!"

Rachel had contemplated revisiting the house, and Maddie's words solidified her decision. "I appreciate your help."

"I'll see you around, Maddie." Rachel waved and headed out of the bakery. Luckily, a taxi was pulling up to the curb. Rachel hopped in and directed the driver back to Mrs. Kincaid's mansion to search for additional clues.

She sat back in the cab, her mind a whirlwind of puzzle pieces, trying to make sense of the clues that had led her this far. The journey had unexpected twists. And now, as the cab pulled in front of the Kincaid imposing mansion, Rachel felt a surge of determination and excitement course through her veins. She could not give up this case—not now or ever.

CHAPTER FIVE

Rachel arrived at the house feeling both determined and overwhelmed. She hastened to the front door, thankful for the serenity of the neighborhood. Although Detective Farley had taken the main set of keys, Rachel had retained one spare front door key for herself. Thus, she was able to let herself in. As she stepped into the living room, Rachel's initial eagerness gave way to a sense of disappointment. Everything appeared to be in its rightful place, except for the askew painting, which she still hadn't adjusted. With a resigned sigh, Rachel pushed away from the door and ventured deeper into the living room. She knew she wouldn't find any clues just by standing at the entrance.

"Where to begin?" she murmured, eyeing the table where she had discovered the coffee cup earlier.

Nothing else seemed amiss. The coffee table lay bare, except for the TV remote, which Mrs. Kincaid usually kept within reach. She would sometimes make her way downstairs with Mr. Arnold to watch TV.

Rachel reached for the remote, intending to return it to its original position on the TV stand. However, in her clumsiness, she accidentally struck her foot against the table, stumbled, and landed on the floor.

"Ow!" Rachel winced as pain shot up her leg. The absence of Mrs. Kincaid's usual admonishments rang hollowly in the room—a stark reminder of her absence, of the fact that someone had taken her life.

The realization spurred Rachel back to her feet. As she scrambled to get up, her gaze fell upon a stain on the carpet. It was a blemish she hadn't noticed before, and she was certain it hadn't been there when she left the house on Saturday night.

Rachel paused, studying the unfamiliar mark, before quickly capturing a photo of it on her phone. She decided to send the image to Detective Farley for further examination. Convinced that there was nothing else worthy to note in the living room, Rachel proceeded to go upstairs to Mrs. Kincaid's office.

Dread tightened its grip on Rachel as she ascended the stairway, and she struggled to shake off the feeling. Since Mrs. Kincaid's death, she hadn't been alone in this house, and the prospect of returning to the scene of the crime filled her with unease. When Rachel reached the hallway, she averted her gaze from Mrs. Kincaid's room, hastening past until she reached the office door, which she promptly entered.

Inside, the scent of lavender lingered more strongly, a testament to the countless hours Mrs. Kincaid had spent here. The office was a modest space, housing a tidy desk, chair, bookcase, and a few paintings adorning the walls, originals no doubt. Rachel walked over to the desk and settled into the plush swivel chair.

The first item to catch her eye, lying prominently in the center of the desk, was Mrs. Kincaid's diary. It was a sleek, black leather journal with an intricate silver clasp, that piqued Rachel's curiosity. She wondered why the police had overlooked it, or if they hadn't yet searched the office.

Rachel knew that if there were any clues to be found, they would likely be contained within the diary. However, a sense of ethical reservation tugged at her. It felt like an invasion of privacy to read the journal of a deceased woman.

She looked around the desk for clues; maybe she wouldn't have to open the diary. After a few minutes of rigorous search, Rachel found nothing.

Nothing was significant on the desk, just books and documents on Mrs. Kincaid's businesses and a few lists of house furniture she wanted to purchase. Mrs.Kincaid was an impulsive spender with enough money to support her habit.

Rachel reached for the diary. Even as she tried to talk herself out of it, she knew she couldn't resist. Her curiosity was too high. She had to peek.

Ignoring every resistance in her heart, she opened the diary. Right in the center of the front page, in red ink, were written two names: Sheila and Pete. Rachel did not read any further.

Her heart slammed in her chest as the significance of what she saw dawned on her. Maybe Luke Farley was right. Maybe one of these two people—no matter how nice they seemed—was responsible for Mrs. Kincaid's death.

Rachel picked up her phone and dialed Detective Farley's number immediately. She had to tell him what she had just seen. The diary might be substantial evidence.

Luke answered promptly. "Hello, Miss Karr?"

"Hello, Luke," Rachel said. "Please, call me Rachel."

"Okay, Rachel. Is there something you need?"

"Have you spoken to Sheila and Pete about Mrs. Kincaid's death?" She asked. "When we met earlier today, you said you would talk to them."

"Uh…not yet. Is there a particular reason you're asking?"

"I just found Mrs. Kincaid's diary, and their names are written on the front page. They might be involved somehow."

Rachel had anticipated Luke's excitement, but his response was lukewarm at best. "Where did you find this diary?" he inquired.

"In Mrs. Kincaid's office." Rachel said softly.

"You are in the house?"

"Yes." Rachel nodded. "I just wanted to-"

"Miss Karr…" Rachel sensed the disapproval in his tone. "I need you to stay away from this. I will handle the investigation as a professional. While you may have provided some clues, that doesn't make you an expert."

"Understood, Luke."

"You must leave the house now! At best, you risk contaminating evidence; at worst, you put yourself in danger. Let's not have this conversation again, please."

"Okay, Detective, On my way out."

With that, he ended the call, and Rachel knew she had upset him. Perhaps he was right. But she understood that all of the house had been cleared.

She rearranged the desk and exited the office.

After shutting the door behind her, Rachel made her way onto the landing towards the stairs, preparing to leave.

Yet, as she passed Mrs. Kincaid's bedroom, a nagging compulsion urged her to search for further clues. If there were more to be found, perhaps they would be here in her bedroom. Just a quick glance wouldn't hurt. She promised herself she wouldn't linger.

With resolve, Rachel entered Mrs. Kincaid's bedroom and closed the door behind her.

CHAPTER SIX

Rachel shut the armoire doors and leaned against it, feeling the ache in her back from bending over for so long. She couldn't determine how much time had passed in this room, but it felt like an eternity.

Every corner had been scrutinized, every speck examined, as Rachel searched for anything that could bolster her case. She wasn't entirely sure what she was seeking, but she trusted her instincts to recognize it if she found it.

As she walked away from the wardrobe to sit on the bed, she heard a strange sound downstairs. It was the unmistakable creak of an opening door. Rachel's heart lurched in her chest, and she tried to convince herself that it was just her imagination. But then, the sound came again—a soft, but distinct, bang of a door closing.

Someone was in the house.

Glancing up at the clock overhead, Rachel gasped when she realized it was past eleven p.m. How had she become so engrossed in her search that she lost track of time? Her mind raced as she listened to the soft footsteps echoing from downstairs. She was growing increasingly nervous with each passing moment.

There was definitely someone else in the house, but they seemed to be downstairs. Who could it be? Could it be the murderer? Bad thoughts were rushing through her mind.

Rachel tiptoed to the door and cautiously opened it, peering out into the hallway before stepping out and silently making her way toward the staircase. When she reached the landing, a gasp escaped her lips. Mr. Arnold stood in front of the painting at the foot of the stairs, his posture remarkably straight. It was a stark departure from his usual hunched demeanor.

Something about the way he stood, hands folded behind his back, sent shivers down Rachel's spine. Before she could react, Mr. Arnold's head snapped in her direction, his eyes widening in surprise.

"Rachel!" he growled, his demeanor suddenly menacing as he began advancing toward her with unexpected speed. Rachel let out a strangled cry and bolted back toward Mrs. Kincaid's room, the sound of Mr. Arnold's footsteps echoing behind her.

Rachel pushed Mrs. Kincaid's door open and ran inside, turning to shut the door behind her. Mr. Arnold was a few steps behind, and she caught a glimpse of the feral expression in his eyes as she closed the door and bolted it. Would she be safe in this fortress?

Rachel reached for her phone on the bed, tears slipping down her face.

Mr. Arnold began to bang on the door. "Open the door, Rachel. I want to talk," he yelled, his voice tinged with urgency.. "It's not what you think."

Ignoring his pleas, Rachel fumbled for the numbers on her phone. Mr. Arnold's relentless banging fueled her panic. She dialed Detective Farley's number, praying for him to pick up.

As the phone rang, Rachel's fears intensified. "Please pick up. Please," she whispered desperately.

Like an answer to her prayer, Luke Farley finally picked up and answered,. "Rachel?"

His voice sounded weary, but Rachel was relieved to hear it. She probably woke him up. "Luke?"

"Rachel? Why are you crying? What's happening?" His tone was now sharper, more focused. "And what's with all that banging?"

"It's Mr. Arnold," Rachel sobbed, the fear evident in her voice. "I'm still in Mrs. Kincaid's house, upstairs in her bedroom. He's trying to break in the locked door. I—I—"

"Crap! Darn it! Rachel! I warned you—" Luke's frustration was noticeable. "I'm on my way. Try to stall him."

Rachel could hear the urgency in Luke's voice, and she knew she had to hold on until he got there.

She clutched her phone tightly, hoping and praying for help to arrive soon.

That door was solid as it was intended to keep out anyone Mrs. Kincaid did not want in. Was it enough?

CHAPTER SEVEN

After her conversation with Luke, Rachel felt a sense of relief. The banging had ceased as soon as she hung up from Luke, and she breathed a sigh of relief. She cautiously approached the bedroom door and pressed her ear against it, relieved to hear only silence. A welcoming sound of a door closing downstairs assured her it was safe now. It seemed Mr. Arnold had left.

Quickly texting Luke to inform him that Mr. Arnold had departed, she received a reassuring response that he was already on his way. Feeling too shaken to leave the room just yet, Rachel decided to wait for Luke to arrive.

About half an hour later, Rachel heard the door open again. She sighed in relief and took a deep breath when she heard Luke's voice calling her. "Rachel."

She finally unlocked the bedroom door and ran out onto the landing. From the landing, she could see Luke standing akimbo in the center of the living room, a young girl beside him. When he saw her coming, a look of concern came into his eyes."Rachel." He walked towards her. "Are you okay?"

"Yes, yes. I'm fine," she smiled.

"Rachel?" Another voice interrupted, and Rachel's eyes widened in recognition. "I know you."

Turning toward the sound, Rachel was surprised to see Maddie standing beside Luke. "Maddie?"

The two embraced, their laughter mingling in the air. "What a coincidence," Maddie remarked, leading Rachel to a nearby couch. "Are you okay?"

"You two know each other?" Luke stared at them in confusion.

Rachel laughed at Luke and turned to Maddie. "This is your father?"

Maddie shared a conspiratorial look with her. "The very one." The two laughed again.

"Maddie?" Luke turned to his daughter with a raised eyebrow. "How do you know Rachel? Have you been snooping around in my business?"

"Dad, chill," Maddie replied, rolling her eyes. "Rachel and I met earlier today at Wonder Express. I didn't even know you two knew each other."

"You just met today?" Luke looked surprised as he turned to Rachel for confirmation. Maddie did not usually bond so quickly with adults. "Do you realize how much danger you put yourself in, Rachel?" His tone was stern, a hint of worry underlying his words. "This is not a game. You could have been seriously hurt."

Rachel nodded, acknowledging the gravity of the situation. "I'm sorry, Luke. I just wanted to help. And Maddie here encouraged me!" She pointed teasingly at Maddie, who couldn't suppress it any longer.

She burst into laughter and raised her arms in surrender. "What? No! I only gave general advice." When she realized that her father's frown wasn't lessening in any way, she rose to her feet. "I'll get Rachel a cup of coffee, if that is cleared and okay, Dad, " Maddie said. Luke nodded. Walking towards the kitchen, she was desperately trying to hide her laugh. She found the automatic coffee pod system ready to go. It was so easy and fun to use.

"I don't think I understand this friendship." Luke pointed in the direction his daughter went. "But you know better than to take advice from a twelve-year-old. And please refrain from telling her anything about the case. I never do."

"I understand," Rachel nodded.

Luke visibly relaxed. "Mr. Arnold has left. I checked his house, but he wasn't there. Did he threaten you in any way?"

"Not really," Rachel told Luke everything that happened. "He just kept banging on the door until he left."

"And he was standing over there when you saw him?" Luke pointed to the landing at the foot of the stairs where the painting was hanging. Rachel nodded. "Yes."

"I spoke to Sheila and Pete today," Luke continued. "They both had alibis. Sheila was out of town visiting her grandkids, and Pete was working late at the bakery."

"He was about to close the bakery at eleven p.m., but a customer came in just as he was ready to close the door. Pete stayed until after she left. He's still on the suspect list," Luke said. "The results from the coffee testing came in. It matched a specimen from Mr. Pete's bakery."

"Wow, I cannot believe this. Mrs. Kincaid never drank coffee that wasn't homemade and especially black." Maddie arrived with a sizzling hot cup of coffee, which she handed Rachel. "Thanks, Maddie."

"You're welcome." Maddie sat down — intrigued by this conversation.

"But what's the big deal with the painting? Everything seems to point back to this." Luke stood from the couch and walked across the living room. Rachel presumed it was to check it out, so she remained seated while sipping her coffee.

A few seconds later, Luke called out to her with an urgency that had her snapping to her feet, the coffee sloshing around in the cup. "Rachel!"

Startled, she looked at Luke. "Yes?"

Luke stood on the landing, holding the painting in his hands. Behind him, where the painting had been, was an open empty safe.

Rachel's eyes widened in realization. "That is a safe!"

Luke nodded, setting the painting down to inspect the empty safe. "Yes. I believe someone poisoned Mrs. Kincaid because they wanted whatever was in here."

"And Mr. Arnold knew about it, too?" Rachel's mind raced as she connected the dots. "That's why he was standing there. He could have been waiting for an opportunity to take whatever was in it."

Luke nodded grimly. "It's possible. But for now, we need to find Mr. Arnold. He and Pete are still on the suspect list, with Mr. Arnold as our prime suspect."

CHAPTER EIGHT

Rachel tossed and turned in bed until daybreak. Despite Luke and Maddie's efforts to ensure her safety, she couldn't shake the events of the night from her mind. Her thoughts raced, circling back to the discovery of the hidden safe behind the painting. It was a revelation that had left her stunned. Why would Mrs. Kincaid conceal something there? And what could possibly be inside?

Her head was full of different thoughts.

First, she was shocked that there was a safe behind the painting. Never once had she tried to move or search behind it. Why should it even cross her mind? But after Luke had discovered it this morning, everything began to make sense. Maybe that was why Mrs. Kincaid spent so much time looking at the painting. It was comforting for her.

What could be in the safe? Whatever it was, Mrs. Kincaid could not reach it, so what was the significance of putting it up there? However, Rachel remembered, Mrs. Kincaid was not in a wheelchair until about ten years ago. Sometimes, a retreat from her bedroom was welcomed to sit on the cozy landing outside her room and have her tea. She could see all over the vast living room.

As morning dawned, Rachel found herself behind the wheel of her car, driving into town with a singular purpose: to speak with Pete. With Sheila having a solid alibi, Pete and Mr. Arnold were the remaining suspects. While Rachel didn't consider herself a detective, she was determined to gather information, hoping it might shed some light on the case.

Pulling up outside the Express, Rachel noticed Pete behind the counter. The shop was still quiet, which suited her intentions perfectly. She greeted Pete with a smile as she approached. "Hi, Pete."

"Rachel, hi." Pete waved enthusiastically. "Good to see you again. How's everything?"

"I'm alright, Pete," Rachel replied. "Back for another slice of that delicious strawberry fudge."

"Well, you're in luck." He laughed. "We have a new batch, straight from the oven."

"M mm." Rachel moaned. "Give me two slices this time."

"Oh, you're going all out." Pete cut the slices a little bigger.

As Pete plated the cake slices, Rachel considered approaching the Kincaid subject with him. She didn't want it to seem like she suspected him, but she also wanted information.

He handed her the plate with a smile."Thank you, Rachel."

"Thanks, Pete." Disappointed in herself, she was about to turn away and leave, but . Pete stopped her.

"Rachel, how are you holding up? I heard about Mrs. Kincaid. Terrible thing."

Rachel seized the opportunity to steer the conversation. "Yes, it's been tough," she replied, feigning innocence. "Did you know her well?"

Pete nodded solemnly. "Yeah, we had our disagreements, but she was a good person at heart. It's a shame what happened."

Rachel nodded sympathetically, allowing Pete to continue. "Seems like my spat with her has put me on the suspect list," Pete remarked with a sigh.

"I'm so sorry to hear that," Rachel said, masking her true intentions.

Pete shrugged, offering a resigned smile. "It's alright. I've got nothing to hide, but it's still uncomfortable. You know, anyone could have been in that house that night."

"Yes, I can only imagine how you feel."Rachel agreed.

"Fortunately, I closed late that night, thanks to the redhead who came in for drinks and a cake slice. Otherwise, I'd have been a strong suspect. Plus, I went straight home after that."

Rachel sighed. She could see his distress, and it would be unfair to probe him further for information. Instead, Rachel reached out to pat his hands. "Don't worry, Pete. Justice will prevail. Okay?" She wrinkled up her nose and smiled.

"Thanks, Rachel. Again, the cakes are on the house."

"Pete, no. How can I—?"

"Please, don't argue with me, young lady." Pete loved to see Rachel enjoy his baked goods, and she was great at testing them.

With a sigh, Rachel thanked him and walked to the seat near the window.

Rachel ate alone while staring outside at the newspaper stand across the street. Like Maddie, this window spot quickly became her favorite in the bakery.

It was still early, so the paper stand was empty. However, watching the vendor arrange the papers sequentially was still fascinating. One could quickly tell he took pride in his job.

She was on her last slice when her phone rang. It was Luke, so she immediately picked up the phone. "Luke?"

"Can you come to the Police station?" Luke's voice was urgent. "There's something you need to know about Mr. Arnold."

"On my way," Rachel replied, quickly finishing her cake and hurrying out of the bakery, waving to Pete as she left.

Arriving at the station, Rachel found Luke waiting for her. His demeanor was serious as he led her to a bench in the reception area.

"Hi, Rachel." Luke unassumingly took her arm as she sat down on the bench. "Why are you breathing so hard?"

"I rushed here and jogged from the car," she answered. "You sounded so urgent."

"Be careful not to get any traffic violations. You are—"

"Luke!" Rachel interrupted him. "What's going on?" Rachel asked, her heart pounding with anticipation.

"Mr. Arnold has been found," Luke began, his expression grave. "He was discovered dead drunk in a saloon near Rainbow Avenue. And when we brought him in, he confessed to killing Mrs. Kincaid."

CHAPTER NINE

Mr. Arnold's confession played over and over in Rachel's mind like a broken record. It had been nearly a week since he admitted to killing Mrs. Kincaid. The village had moved on, the police had closed the case, and everyone seemed ready to put the tragic event behind them. But Rachel couldn't shake the feeling that something was amiss.

"There was a lot of money in her safe behind the painting on the wall. She told me about it whenever I visited and planned to use it as her retirement fund in a few years. I don't know what came over me, but I'd planned to steal it for months. I finally got to do it that Saturday. When she needed to get into the safe, I was the one to help her. She trusted me. I gave her the orange juice, and she drank it."

As she listened to the recording once more, she couldn't help but feel that Mr. Arnold's slurred confession lacked conviction. It was too vague, too rehearsed.

If he were guilty, the story given by Mr. Arnold would be more assertive and less bland. He didn't explain anything, nor did he give vivid details. He confessed and clammed up. All other efforts to talk him into revealing more were in vain. Because Mr. Arnold admitted to killing Mrs. Kincaid, and everyone wanted to move on, the Police arrested him and marked the case solved.

Rachel told Luke her concerns about the confession, but he rightfully explained that he was just a part of the system. He couldn't do any more than what they wanted, and had no choice if the Department's top gun said to pack it up. Mrs. Kincaid's body was also released in preparation for her cremation.

Anne called earlier this morning to let Rachel know she was coming to Bel Harbor with Jessica. Anne said arrangements were completed. Mrs. Kincaid's body would be cremated, and the house sold. Jessica wanted nothing to do with the home or Bel Harbor, and Rachel wondered what must have happened between mother and daughter to cause such a wide rift that was unforgivable, even in death.

Her phone rang as she was again about to play Mr. Arnold's confession.

It was Anne. "Hello, Rachel."

"Hi, Anne. Are you in Bel Harbor already?"

"That's why I called," Anne said. "I'm so sorry to bother you. Jessica and I just arrived at the house, and it's locked. Do you have a key?"

The primary keys to the house were with the Police, but Rachel still had her spare. "I have one," she said. "I'll bring it to you."

"Thank you so much, Rachel. You're a lifesaver," Anne said gratefully.

"It's no problem at all," Rachel reassured them. The house was cleared and all the tape removed. "If you need anything else, just give me a call."

Rachel could call Luke and deliver the primary keys to the ladies, but that would be boring. How could she pass up the opportunity to see Anne and meet Jessica?

She had an idea of how Anne would look from hearing her voice numerous times, especially since the death of Mrs. Kincaid. However, she had no idea how Jessica looked. Would she look like her mother?

Would she have the same crabby attitude? Or would she be sunny and friendly like Anne?

She would find out soon enough as she neared the house. There was a Volvo parked by the curb and two ladies standing in front of the Kincaid mansion. Both were blonde. One was smiling and talking while the other listened quietly. Rachel guessed the quiet one was Jessica. She had Mrs. Kincaid's nose.

She parked her car close to the Volvo and got out, holding the key. "Are you Rachel?" The smiling lady walked down the porch towards her. Rachel noticed the cute mole on her jaw. I'm Anne." She touched her chest. "It's so nice to meet you." Anne hugged Rachel. "I'm sure you must have been so busy when I called you. Thank you for coming out."

"Yes. I'm Rachel. It's not a problem." Rachel handed the key over to Anne.

"Jess!" Anne motioned to the other lady standing on the porch. "This is Rachel, your Mama's caregiver. She took excellent care of her. It gave me some free time."

"It's nice to meet you, Rachel," Jess said coolly. "Thanks for everything."

"You're welcome." Rachel turned to Anne. "I have to leave now. If you need anything, please give me a call."

"Sure." Anne hugged her again. "Take care, Rachel. I'm sure this must be hard for you, too."

As Rachel turned to leave, she noticed a strand of red hair peeking out from beneath Anne's blonde wig. Initially, Rachel had assumed the blonde hair was Anne's natural color, given how seamlessly it complemented her complexion. But up close, it was evident that it was a wig. Perhaps Anne was having a bad hair day after the long journey—it was a seven-hour drive, after all.

Rachel got into her car and started the ignition, but she found herself lost in thought. The sight of Anne's wig sparked a curiosity within her. She pondered the idea of getting a wig or perhaps even dyeing her hair. After all, she had sported her dark red hair for her entire life; maybe it was time for a change. Lost in contemplation, Rachel continued her journey home.

Suddenly, memories from a previous conversation flooded her mind, causing her heart to race. She slammed on the brakes, the realization hitting her like a ton of bricks. Without hesitation, Rachel made a sharp U-turn and headed straight to Wonder Express. This time, Pete wasn't behind the counter. Instead, it was Berry, Pete's wife, who greeted her warmly.

"Hi, Berry. Is Pete around?"

"Why, yes. He's in the kitchen," Berry answered, her voice filled with curiosity. "Are you alright?"

"Yes, I just have some important questions to ask. Can I see Pete, please?" Rachel shifted from one foot to the other, feeling a surge of urgency.

"Okay, sure. Take a seat over there," Berry gestured towards one of the empty seats in the shop. "I'll see if he can pop out for a few seconds."

Rachel took the offered seat while Berry disappeared into the kitchen. When Pete appeared a few minutes later, Rachel's heart skipped a beat.

"Is everything okay, Rachel?" Pete asked, walking around the counter towards her.

"Everything is fine, Pete," she smiled. "I just have a few questions, please."

Pete sat across the table from her, his brows furrowing in concentration. "I'm listening."

"Pete, do you remember the redhead who came to buy drinks from you the night Mrs. Kincaid died? You mentioned it to me the last time I was here."

"Oh," Pete frowned, deep in thought. "Uh…she was the last customer of the day. I think I remember her because she had vivid red hair. I haven't seen that in a while. Also, she bought chamomile tea along with her cup of coffee. The only other person I know that drank that tea was Mrs. Kincaid to help her sleep."

"Do you remember what the redhead looked like?" Rachel pressed on, her patience wearing thin.

"Uh…" Pete slowly shook his head. "I'm not sure."

"Do you have a CCTV camera?" Rachel's excitement grew. Her instincts were urging her to uncover the truth, and she needed Pete's help to do so.

"No. I've not gotten around to that."

"Pete!" Rachel exclaimed in frustration. "You've had your bakery for fifteen years. You should get cameras."

"I know. I know. Who is this girl?" Pete frowned. "Did she do something?"

Rachel leaned forward, her excitement rising. "Pete, please try to remember something besides her red hair. Is she tall?"

"Just average height, like you, but on the bigger size," Pete recalled, his face brightening as a memory surfaced.

Rachel felt a surge of triumph. "Yes!"She"exclaimed inwardly, leaning back against the chair. She didn't have all the information, but she knew she was onto something.

"Oh…" Pete's face lit up as realization dawned. "She had a mole on her jaw. Right here," he touched his jaw, recalling the detail vividly. "I saw it as she was leaving."

"Thank you so much, Pete! You are the best!" Rachel hugged him briefly, gratitude flooding her, before rushing out of the bakery. She got into her car and headed straight for the Police Station.

CHAPTER TEN

Rachel entered Luke's office breathlessly, her heart pounding with urgency. "It was Anne who killed Mrs. Kincaid. Not Mr. Arnold."

"What?" Luke's eyes widened as he stared at Rachel from across his desk. "Anne? Are you sure of everything you're saying?"

"Absolutely!"

Luke ran a tired hand down his face, his brow furrowing in deep thought. "Rachel, if I act on this and you're wrong, it could spell trouble for both of us. We've already closed the case at the office, and Mr. Arnold is in custody."

"But he didn't do it, Luke," Rachel insisted. "You know he didn't. Anne is the one responsible."

"I know." Luke nodded. "But how can we be certain Anne did it?"

"Luke," Rachel slapped a hand on the table. "She did it. Think about it. She knew about whatever was in that safe because she's the only relative who ever came around. She could have easily gained access to the house and the safe. It all fits!"

Luke stayed quiet for a few seconds until he suddenly rose. "Then let's go pay Anne a visit. But we have to tread carefully."

Luke and Rachel were on their way to the Kincaid house within half an hour. The plan was to invite Anne to the station for questioning rather than making an immediate arrest, considering the potential consequences if they were wrong.

The ride to the house was tense, and doubts began to gnaw at Rachel's mind as they approached.

She was the reason they were heading to the Kincaid mansion, and Luke was staking his career on her theory. What if she was wrong? But the evidence seemed clear. Anne was in Bel Harbor, she had access to the house, and Pete's description matched her. Anne was in Bel Harbor!

Eventually, they arrived at the Kincaid house and got out of the vehicle. As they walked toward the front door, Rachel could feel the weight of responsibility bearing down on her. She exchanged a glance with Luke, and he seemed to understand her apprehension. Taking a deep breath, Rachel knocked.

"Who is it?" Anne's voice came from inside the house.

"It's Rachel."

"Oh, Rachel," Anne opened the door. "It's so nice to—"

"Good evening, Anne." Luke interrupted, flashing his badge. "I'm Detective Farley. I'm here to—"

Before Luke could finish, Anne slammed the door shut, leaving them outside. Luke was momentarily taken aback, but he quickly regained his composure, drew his gun, and pushed the door open.

Anne stood in the kitchen doorway, a gun held to Jessica's back.

"Drop your gun," Anne shouted at Luke," The usual friendliness in her eyes was gone. "Or I'll kill her."

"Anne?" Jessica's voice trembled, confusion and fear evident on her face. "Will someone tell me what's going on?"

Luke watched Anne carefully, while he secured his own weapon in the back of his waistband.

"Anne!" Luke approached cautiously, raising his hands. "Let her go. I came to invite you to the station for questioning. That's all."

"No!" Anne shook her head vehemently. Rachel couldn't believe the transformation in Anne's demeanor. Just hours ago, this woman had hugged her with warmth and kindness.

"It was you, Anne, wasn't it?" Rachel interjected.

Anne glanced at Rachel. "How did you know?"

"The red hair poking out from that wig. Pete described the vivid red hair and the mole on your cheek. You were in the Express late that night and left with a coffee and chamomile tea. You mistakenly left one of Pete's coffee cups on the table here," Rachel explained, her voice steady with conviction.

"Rachel, don't engage," Luke warned. "Let me handle this."

"The red hair, then?" Anne yanked the blonde wig from her head, revealing a mane of beautiful red hair. It was as vivid as Pete described.

"Anne," Jessica asked. "What did you do? Please tell me what's going on?"

"I killed your Mama. That's what is going on!" Anne burst into tears, but her hold on Jessica didn't budge.

"What?" Jessica's eyes widened in shock.

"Yes! You have always had a good life!" Anne cried. "You've had everything I wanted: the money, the life, the men, everything!"

"Anne!" Jessica's voice cracked with disbelief..

"When you and your Mama had that ugly disagreement years ago, I chose to be there for her. I always called her once a month, but you never did. You forgot about her completely. You never checked up on her to see if she was okay, Jessica; I did all that.

Yet, when writing her will, she dedicated all her wealth to you while I get nothing, not even this wretched house, which I could have sold for much more than I took out of that safe."

Jessica began to cry. "She was my mom! You couldn't have loved her more than I did! Nothing can change that."

"Well, she's dead now!" Anne's callous words caused Jessica to sob uncontrollably.

Suddenly, Rachel pushed hard against Anne and kicked her thigh, causing her hold on Jessica to weaken.

Taking advantage of the distraction, Jessica broke free and ran toward Luke, who quickly ushered her to safety. Meanwhile, Rachel and Luke aimed their guns at Anne.

"Anne," Luke's voice was firm. "What was in that safe?" He gestured toward the painting covering the empty safe on the wall.

"Two hundred thousand dollars cash." Anne shrugged, defeat evident in her eyes. "Since I knew she wasn't leaving anything to me in her will, I decided to take it. I needed the money. I deserved a good life like Jessica's."

"So you killed my mom for that!" Jessica yelled.

"Oh, stop it. It wasn't like you treasured your Mama," Anne retorted. "She didn't suffer, I assure you. When I called to tell her I was coming, she asked me to stop by Wonder Express and buy her chamomile tea. It was almost midnight, and she said it would help her sleep. I poisoned the tea before giving it to her in her favorite teacup."

"Oh, God." Jessica's cries turned into anguished wails. "I could have helped you, Anne. I would have shared my money, my inheritance—anything with you. She did not have to die this way."

"What about Mr. Arnold?" Luke pressed. "What do you know about him?"

"He was in the house and came into the room while I was taking the money out of the safe. He didn't know Mrs. Kincaid was dead. I was not supposed to be in Bel Harbor." Anne sniffed. "But I threatened to harm his children if he ever told anyone I was there. His children, Jack and Willy, are my neighbors back in the city."

"Anne!" Luke shook his head in disbelief. "You are under arrest for the murder of Mrs. Kincaid. You have the right to remain silent. Anything you say can and will be used against you in court."

Anne collapsed to the floor, her sobs echoing through the room. Rachel and Luke exchanged a relieved glance.

It was finally over.

CONCLUSION

Anne awaits trial, her remorse apparent.

Mr. Arnold is released and is a very thankful and happy man.

Detective Luke, not liking loose ends, contacts Mr. Arnold to ask about the substance he put in Mrs. Kincaid's orange juice. It was from a pill case marked "PM" in her bathroom, which he thought was a sleeping pill. He crushed one and put it in her orange juice to gain access to the safe later that night. Upon hearing of Mrs. Kincaid's death, fearing he had overdosed her, he disappeared. But realizing he had done nothing wrong, he decided to turn himself in.

For closure, Rachel visits the Kincaid mansion one last time. She retrieves the pill case, which she knows so well, and finds that the Police have already examined it. Inside, she discovers Mrs. Kincaid's pain medication, marked "PM" for nighttime use. Mrs. Kincaid had simply forgotten to take it—so no harm was done to her, and there was nothing to rob in the safe. Mr. Arnold's only crime was not telling them about seeing Anne.

Detective Luke and all his Precinct, are relieved to have closure. Chief Payne, and the higher-ups are shocked by the turn of events—a major case solved by an amateur sleuth.

Finally, Rachel has the answers to the questions that plagued her while listening to Mr. Arnold's confession recordings. She couldn't believe Mr. Arnold was guilty, and now she knows the truth.

THE HAPPY ENDING

Presently, tranquility returns to the village of Bel Harbor. Residents resume their pursuits, and Jessica claims her inheritance. It is substantially more than anyone expected.

Mr. Arnold performs his community service happily, forming a close friendship with Miss Sheila.

Mr. Pete and Berry continue to run the bakery, serving heavenly snacks until midnight.

Detective Luke returns to his routine, enjoying time with Maddie as she grows into a teenager. He is also enjoying the friendship developing with Rachel.

Rachel receives offers to be a caretaker from wealthy residents but decides to pursue her dream of owning an antique shop. She will still engage with people but will enjoy a break from amateur sleuthing until the next unexpected opportunity arises.

See you in the next book!

Emma Lenn

If you liked this short introductory novella,

Mayhem Murder and Midnight Tea, A Bel Harbor Cozy Mystery

then you will love the next three books.

Follow Rachel, Luke, and Maddie—a fantastic trio—in the next novels.

Link: https://www.amazon.com/dp/BOCYDSQK9B

Book 2	*Books, Burglars, and a Body, A Bel Harbor Cozy Mystery*

Burglars steal a rare and priceless book from the Bel Harbor Library. In the serene, affluent village, chaos brews beneath the surface. When a murder is committed, the mystery unfolds, sending ripples throughout this small town.

Rachel Karr and Detective Luke kick into high gear to solve this puzzling case.

https://www.amazon.com/dp/BOC2NPP554

Book 3 | *Deadly Double Deception, A Bel Harbor Cozy Mystery*

In the shadow of the tranquil and picturesque Bel Harbor Village, beyond the sleepy Bel River, lies the pulsating and vibrant heart of the notorious Financial District—a realm teeming with double lives, love, lies, latent dangers, and death. Behind the facade of bustling activity, double deception lurks in the background. Mysteries and secrets simmer beneath the surface.

The lives of four people hang in the balance: Henry, Elizabeth, James and Andrea.

Rachel Karr, amateur sleuth, joins Detective Farley and his daughter to form a formidable trio to try to solve this intriguing mystery.

https://www.amazon.com/dp/B0D8HC32YV

Links:

https://www.amazon.com/dp/B0D91ZHJ4

Book 4 | *Scandalous Secrets, and Skeletons,, A Bel Harbor Cozy Mystery*

The whisper of secrets and echoes of scandalous intrigue beckons, and the clatter of skeletons clamor for truth and liberation.

All this commotion keeps the little town of Bel Harbor in shockwaves.

The curious locals ride out a roller coaster of thrilling adventure, where every corner holds a clue and every smile hides a mystery.

It takes all the skill of the fantastic trio: Rachel, Luke, and Maddie to solve this case.

Made in the USA
Monee, IL
16 October 2024

68096302R00036